P9-DGX-504

FORTUNATELY

Written and illustrated by
REMY CHARLIP

Aladdin Paperbacks

Aladdin Paperbacks
An imprint of Simon & Schuster
Children's Publishing Division
1230 Avenue of the Americas
New York, NY 10020
Copyright © 1964 by Remy Charlip
All rights reserved including the right of reproduction in whole or in part in any form.
First Aladdin Paperbacks edition, 1993
Also available in a hard cover edition from Simon & Schuster Books for Young Readers
Manufactured in China
20

Library of Congress Cataloging-in-Publication Data
Charlip, Remy.
  Fortunately / written and illustrated by Remy Charlip.—1st Aladdin Books ed.
    p.   cm.
  Summary: Good and bad luck accompany Ned from New York to Florida on his way to a surprise party.
  ISBN 0-689-71660-5
  [1. Luck—Fiction.]   I. Title.
[PZ7.C3812Fo   1993]
[E]—dc20   92-22794

THIS BOOK IS DEDICATED TO NED AND CLAUDE AND THE PAPER BAG PLAYERS

Fortunately
one day, Ned got a letter that said,
"Please Come to a Surprise Party."

But unfortunately
the party was in Florida
and he was in New York.

*Fortunately
a friend loaned him an airplane.*

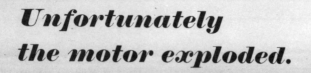

Unfortunately
the motor exploded.

Fortunately
there was a parachute in the airplane.

**Unfortunately
there was a hole in the parachute.**

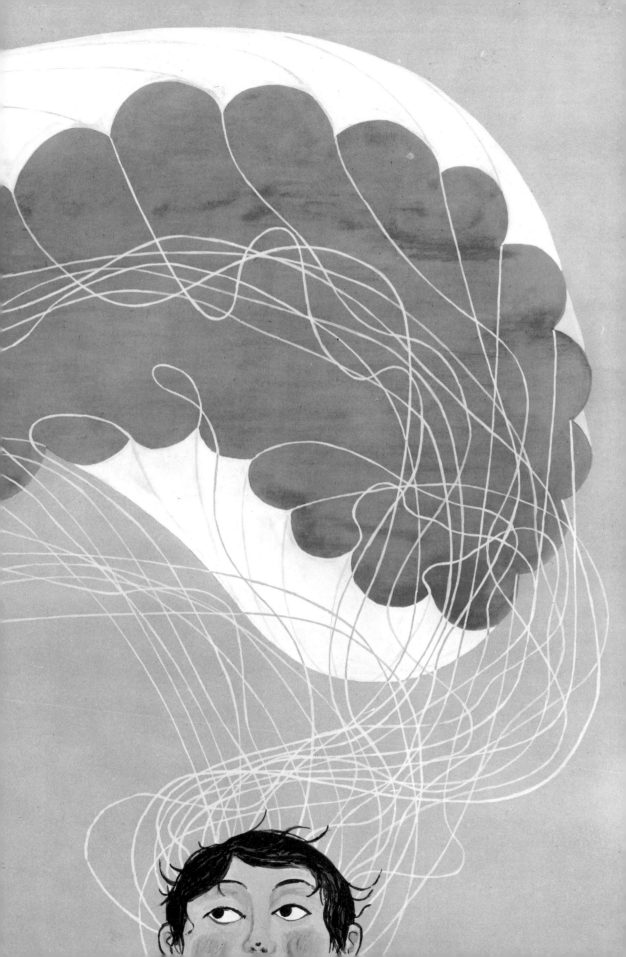

**Fortunately
there was a haystack on the ground.**

Unfortunately
there was a pitchfork in the haystack.

**Fortunately
he missed the pitchfork.**

**Unfortunately
he missed the haystack.**

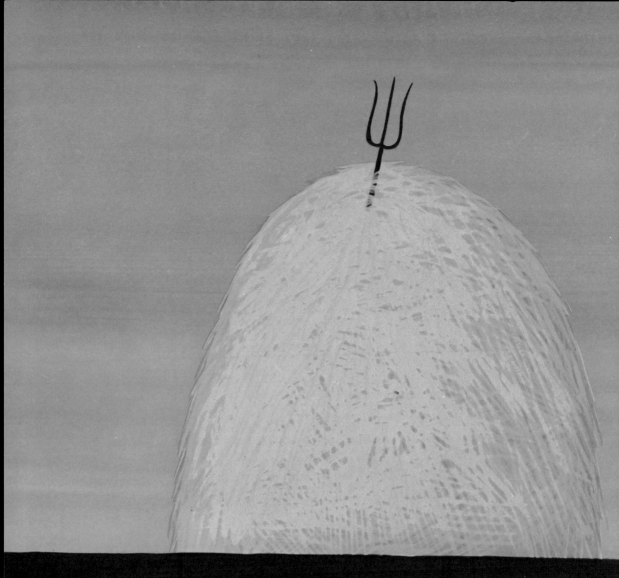

**Fortunately
he landed in water.**

Unfortunately
there were sharks in the water.

Fortunately
he could swim.

Unfortunately
there were tigers on the land.

Fortunately
he could run.

Unfortunately
he ran into a deep dark cave.

**Fortunately
he could dig.**

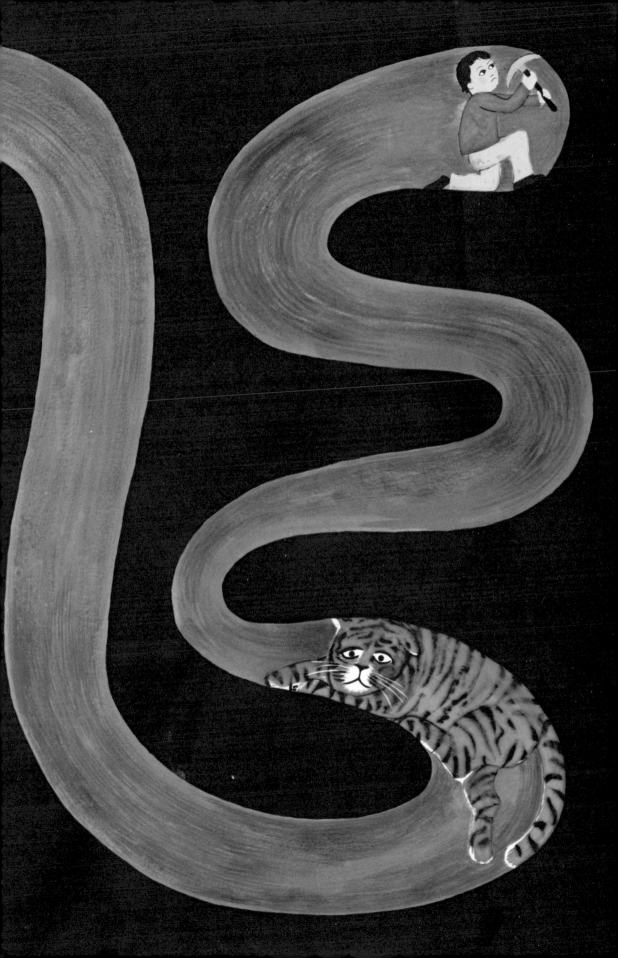

*Unfortunately
he dug himself into a fancy ballroom.*

**Fortunately
there was a surprise party going on.
And fortunately
the party was for him,
because fortunately
it was his birthday!**